Books by Ron Glick:

Godslayer Cycle
One
Two
Three (*July, 2015*)

Chaos Rising
Tarinel's Song
Immortal's Discord (*July, 2014*)

Oz – Wonderland
The Wizard In Wonderland
Dorothy Through the Looking Glass
The Wonderful Alice of Oz (*January, 2015*)

Trivia Books
Ron El's Comic Book Trivia Volume 1
Ron El's Comic Book Trivia Volume 2
Ron El's Comic Book Trivia Volume 3
Ron El's Comic Book Trivia Volume 4
Ron El's Comic Book Trivia Volume 5
Ron El's Comic Book Trivia Volume 6
Ron El's Comic Book Trivia Volume 7
Ron El's Comic Book Trivia Volume 8
Ron El's Comic Book Trivia Volume 9
Ron El's Comic Book Trivia Volume 10
Ron El's Comic Book Trivia Volume 11 (*July, 2014*)

In Dedication

jutopia of The Settlers Online
The first lady three-time champ of CBT

Copyright © Ron Glick, 2014
"Ron El" and "Ron El's Comic Book Trivia" ™ Ron Glick, 2012-2014
ISBN: 1499324251 - ISBN13: 978-1499324259

FOREWARD

COMIC BOOKS, BY THEIR VERY NATURE, REPRESENT THE CONGLOMERATION OF COUNTLESS OF CREATIVE MINDS. AN INDIVIDUAL CHARACTER MIGHT BE CREATED BY ONE OR PERHAPS A FEW PEOPLE, BUT IF THE CHARACTER HAS ANY KIND OF LONGEVITY, MORE OFTEN THAN NOT, THIS WILL MEAN THAT OTHER MINDS BESIDES HIS OR HER CREATORS WILL BE INVOLVED IN SHAPING THE WORLD THE CHARACTER MOVES THROUGH.

ALONG THE WAY, NOT ONLY DO THESE CHARACTERS GROW, BUT THEY ALSO EVOLVE. SOMETIMES, THE ORIGINAL CHARACTERS ARE EVEN REPLACED BY ENTIRELY NEW PEOPLE - A MANTLE MAY BE PASSED, A NEW COSTUME MIGHT BE CREATED, OR EVEN A NEW SUPER IDENTITY ESTABLISHED. IN ESSENCE, THE VERY FABRIC OF COMIC BOOKS HAS ALWAYS BEEN EXEMPLIFIED BY THE DIVERSITY OF CHANGE WITHIN THE FICTIONAL WORLDS THESE CHARACTERS MOVE THROUGH.

I WAS RECENTLY INVOLVED IN A DISCUSSION THAT TOUCHED UPON THIS TOPIC. FELICIA DAY, ARGUABLY THE LEADING QUEEN OF GEEKDOM HERSELF, WEIGHED IN ON THE DISCUSSION OF WHETHER IT WAS PROPER FOR A WHITE ACTOR OR ACTRESS

TO PLAY A RACIAL ROLE, AND THAT THIS WAS NOT EQUIVALENT TO A TRADITIONAL WHITE ROLE BEING RECAST TO BE PLAYED BY AN ETHNIC INDIVIDUAL. FELICIA SPECIFICALLY WAS CITING THE PROTESTS REVOLVING AROUND THE ROLE OF TIGER LILY BEING GIVEN TO ROONEY MARA (A LOVELY, THOUGH DECIDEDLY WHITE ACTRESS) IN THE UPCOMING WARNER BROS. MOVIE, PAN, AS COMPARED TO THE CASTING OF MICHAEL B. JORDAN AS THE HUMAN TORCH. HER POSITION WAS THAT THE FIRST WAS UNACCEPTABLE, BUT THE LATTER REPRESENTED A RE-IMAGINING OF THE CLASSIC FANTASTIC FOUR MEMBER.

MY OWN INITIAL ENTRY INTO THIS DEBATE WAS ESSENTIALLY IN AGREEMENT WITH FELICIA. I MYSELF BOYCOTTED THE LONE RANGER BECAUSE JOHNNY DEPP - A NON-NATIVE ACTOR - WAS CAST AS TONTO (HE IN FACT HAD TO WEAR FACE PAINT THROUGH THE ENTIRE MOVIE TO HIDE THIS FACT). I PERSONALLY FEEL THAT THE EFFORT TO CAST WHITE ACTORS OR ACTRESSES IN ETHNIC ROLES (KEEPING IN MIND THAT THEY ARE *STILL* SUPPOSED TO BE THE SPECIFIC RACE, EVEN THOUGH THE ACTORS CLEARLY ARE NOT) IS AKIN TO THE GREASE MAKEUP WORN BY STAGE PERFORMERS PRETENDING TO BE BLACK MEN IN THE EARLY TWENTIETH CENTURY - IT IS DISRESPECTFUL AND IT HAS NO PLACE IN ENTERTAINMENT, IN MY HUMBLE OPINION.

I DID HOWEVER BRANCH AWAY ON ONE KEY POINT - I DID NOT BELIEVE THAT JOHNNY STORM SHOULD HAVE BEEN CAST AS A LONE BLACK CHARACTER IN THE UPCOMING FANTASTIC FOUR MOVIE. MY REASONING IS NOT THAT I BELIEVE JOHNNY STORM COULD NOT BE RE-IMAGINED AS A BLACK MAN - IT IS THAT THEY SPECIFICALLY CAST A WHITE ACTRESS, KATE MARA (SISTER, IRONICALLY ENOUGH, OF ROONEY MARA MENTIONED ABOVE), TO PLAY SUSAN STORM. PERSONALLY, I WOULD HAVE LOVED TO SEE THE STORM SIBLINGS BOTH CAST AS BLACK, IF FOR NO OTHER REASON THAN - PRESUMABLY - SUE AND REED WOULD STILL EVENTUALLY MARRY AND BE A CORNERSTONE OF INTERRACIAL MARRIAGE IN MARVEL'S FIRST FAMILY. HOWEVER, I GREATLY OBJECT TO THE IDEA OF CASTING JOHNNY STORM AS BLACK *JUST* TO HAVE A BLACK CHARACTER IN THE MOVIE, WHICH IS WHERE I SEE THIS DECISION.

AS IT STANDS, I DO NOT CONCEIVE OF A METHOD TO HAVE THE STORM SIBLINGS *BE* SIBLINGS IN THE NEW FANTASTIC FOUR REBOOT UNLESS ONE OR THE OTHER IS NOW ADOPTED OR THAT THEY ARE HALF-SIBLINGS. AND THIS UNDERMINES THE EXCEPTIONALLY CLOSE BOND THE TWO HAVE ALWAYS HAD IN THE COMICS. THE PRODUCERS OF THE NEW MOVIE COULD HAVE CAST REED RICHARDS AS BLACK AND IT WOULD NOT HAVE RAISED AN EYEBROW

FOR ME. BUT TO SPLIT UP A FAMILY, EVEN A FICTIONAL ONE, JUST TO HAVE A TOKEN RACE CARD PLAYED? THIS I JUST CANNOT STOMACH.

AGAIN, I HAVE NO OBJECTION TO CHARACTERS BEING RE-IMAGINED FOR THE MOVIES AS RACIALLY DIVERSE - I LIKED THE CASTING OF IDRIS ELBA AS HEIMDALL IN THOR, FOR EXAMPLE. I THOUGHT THAT HE DID A FRANKLY AWESOME JOB IN THE ROLE. AND, AS I HAVE MENTIONED, DIVERSITY AND EVOLUTION ARE KEY COMPONENTS OF THE CONSTANTLY EXPANDING COMIC BOOK CANVAS. BUT I AM SORRY - I HAVE TO PROTEST WHEN A MAJOR MEDIA FRANCHISE JUST WANTS A BLACK MAN IN THEIR MOVIE AS A TOKEN MINORITY FIGURE.

I HATE TO SAY IT, BUT I PLAN TO BOYCOTT THIS FILM. I AM ALL FOR MODERNIZING CHARACTERS IN MEDIA, BUT LET US DO IT IN A RESPECTFUL AND - MOST IMPORTANTLY - PURPOSEFUL WAY.

WE ARE ALL A PART OF HISTORY HERE. I SAY LET US LEAVE A BETTER EXAMPLE THAN THIS BEHIND.

RON GLICK
APRIL 29, 2014

RON EL'S COMIC BOOK TRIVIA
VOLUME 10

1. What comic book title prompted a lawsuit from New Kids On the Block?

Answer

Rock N Roll Comics – Revolutionary Comics published unauthorized biographies in comic book form through their title, Rock N Roll Comics, and though most artists featured were supportive, the New Kids On the Block sued, claiming that the comics were essentially bootlegs of their work – though the United States District Court of California disagreed.

2. What villain cloned Marvel's first family and sent the clones after their first enemy?

Answer

Aron, aka, the Rogue Watcher – The Watcher race set themselves up as observers of cosmic events, but Aron renounced his race's purpose to act as a nemesis of existence and the Fantastic Four specifically, going so far at one point as to clone the foursome in an effort to cast his enemies as villains, starting off with a vicious attack against their first superhuman opponent, the Mole Man.

3. Who stole residual energy left over with people saved by a hero in order to resurrect his wife?

Answer

David Hersch, aka, Cicada - Hersch gained the ability to absorb the life energies of others after being struck by lightning, which also gave him a vision of his murdered wife being resurrected - yet when his plot to steal the energies left over with all those saved by Wally West, aka, Flash III, as well as the Flash's own energies, succeeded in bringing his wife back to life, she revealed that he been the one to murder her, compelling the villain to take her life once more.

4. What superteam consists of vampires who have overcome their need for human blood?

Answer

The Forgiven - The Japanese vampire, Raizo Kodo, learned how to overcome his own need for human blood and helped the members of the team he gathered to do the same, going on to lead his team notably in lending assistance in defending Dracula from an attack by a Nul-possessed Hulk and teaching the vampire-tainted X-Man, Jubilee, the skills necessary to overcome her own bloodlust.

5. What universe-altering event was caused by the compression of time making characters from alternate realities appear?

Answer

Zero Hour - The Zero Hour crisis was DC Comics' effort to fix the chronology problems created by re-writing their universe following the Crisis on Infinite Earths, and was initially evidenced inside the storyline by witnessing alternate versions of characters not in consistency with the present time-line culminating in the DC Universe actually fading out of existence towards the end of the series.

6. What prison facility was originally used to house eleven members of a superhero team?

Answer

The Vault, aka, United States Maximum Security Installation for the Incarceration of Superhuman Criminals – Though the facility was better known over the years prior to its destruction as a facility for detaining super-powered criminals, its first inhabitants were actually eleven members of the Avengers West and East Coast teams, who at the time were suspected of treason.

7. What being was created through bonding with the Sentience of the Universe just prior to his universe's destruction?

Answer

Galan, aka, Galactus – Known as the Devourer of Worlds, Galactus is actually the sole survivor of the universe that existed before the Big Bang, having been consumed in his universe's destruction known as the Big Crunch, but somehow spared when the living embodiment of his universe bonded with him as he was being consumed, leaving him gestating through the Big Bang and eventually to emerge as a cosmic force for destruction in the new universe.

8. What heroine began her crime fighting career because her father's life-long goal of training her for the police force was turned down?

Answer

Dinah Drake, aka, Dinah Drake Lance, aka, Black Canary I - In the Post-Crisis DC Universe, Black Canary was split between two generations of heroines - mother and daughter - with the mother, Dinah Drake, being trained by her detective father to continue the family tradition by joining the police department - only to have the police department ultimately reject Dinah's application.

9. What Frenchman worked undercover in occupied France during World War II using the letter "V" to inspire the citizens against Nazi occupation?

Answer

John Watkins, aka, Citizen V - As a British officer, Watkins was reported killed in action, but his superiors saw an opportunity to use his reported death as a way of imbedding him into Nazi controlled France during World War II, where he adopted the name Citizen V ("V" for Victory), leaving his stylized V behind on his various adventures to give the resistance a symbol to rally around.

10. What hero threatened to substitute documents to fully take over another man's life if he were not permitted to assume his identity voluntarily?

Answer

Kent Allard, aka, the Shadow – Allard discovered an extremely close resemblance to the man Lamont Cranston, and began to impersonate Cranston as a simulated secret identity when the real Cranston was out of town – but when Cranston confronted Allard over the ruse, Allard threatened to completely take over Cranston's life and assets unless the real man continued to allow him to assume the faux identity while Cranston was out traveling the world, a threat Cranston had no choice but to accept.

11.   What character's grisly demise inspired a list circulated through the Internet of female characters who had been killed, depowered or injured?

Answer

Alex DeWitt – When Alex DeWitt, the girlfriend of Green Lantern Kyle Rainer, was murdered and stuffed into a refrigerator by Major Force, it led to comic book writer Gail Simone assembling a list known as "Women In Refrigerators", a list comprised of fictional female characters who had been injured, killed or depowered with the intent of examining the disproportionate use of females being victimized as plot devices in comics.

12.   What Asgardian's attack inspired the legend for Little Red Riding Hood?

Answer

Fenris Wolf – Said to be the progeny of Loki and the giantess, Angrboda, Fenris attempted to attack the goddess, Iduna, in order to steal her Golden Apples of Immortality destined for All-Father Odin, but he is driven away by Haakun the Hunter and banished to the shadow-realm of Varinheim – a story that acted as the foundation for the legend of Little Red Riding Hood forever after.

13.What villain was sired from a rape by a sorcerer's son upon his cousin on her wedding night?

Answer

Kordax – The source of the Curse of Kordax superstition – where Atlanteans born with blonde hair are presumed cursed and often left to the elements at birth – Kordax was born of the rape from Dardanus, son of the mad sorcerer Shalako, upon the princess, Cora, his cousin whom he had an incestuous love for since they were children.

14.   What superhero's identity - known by a first name of a single letter - lasted for only for his premier issue before changing it?

Answer

Doug Danville, aka, K the Unknown, aka, Black Owl I - Danville was a millionaire playboy who was simply tired of being a playboy, so put on a costume to fight crime - but his first foray only lasted for one adventure as K the Unknown before he changed his secret identity to the Black Owl with his second appearance without explanation.

15.   Who was transformed into a heavily muscled alter ego when she found a discarded Asgardian axe?

Answer

Jackie Lukus, aka, Bloodaxe – Originally concealed from even the audience, the identity of this villain was a mystery for quite awhile after a showy figure found the discarded axe of the Agardian villain, the Executioner, and found herself transformed into the powerhouse known as Bloodaxe, all the while the secret identity of this new villain being Jackie Lukus, the love interest of Eric Masterson, aka, Thunderstrike.

16. What superteam was founded by Thomas Wayne after his wife and son were killed?

Answer

Justice League (Elseworlds) – In a world where Superman and Batman never existed, Bruce Wayne brought together his own version of the Justice League to eliminate crime in Gotham City, though he eventually decided to branch out nationwide with super powered members after the Human Bomb exploded in a hotel, killing the United States Cabinet in the process.

17.   What comic book romance inspired the wife of a rock star to attempt to make a television series out of the comic couple?

Answer

Black Widow and Daredevil – In the 1970s, Daredevil's relationship with Black Widow evolved to the point where he agreed to move with her out of New York and to San Francisco when the star duo gained the attention of Angela Bowie – wife of David Bowie – who decided to use it as a springboard into her own acting career by pitching to make the romantic couple into a television show, with herself as the female lead – an effort that obviously failed.

18.   What insane asylum was inspired by a horror author's fictional community in Massachusetts?

Answer

The Elizabeth Arkham Asylum For the Criminally Insane, aka, Arkham Asylum – Many of H.P. Lovecraft's books were based in the fictional town of Arkham, Massachusetts, and though the asylum of the same name was given from the founder Amadeus Arkham's family name, the true inspiration for Dennis O'Neil's creation of the infamous home for the criminally insane came from Lovecraft's demonic community.

19.   Who shattered reality by breaking a
magical lasso?

Answer

Rama Khan – The immortal villain was challenged by the Justice League in a conflict where he broke Wonder Woman's lasso, resulting in a cosmic backlash that resulted in reality being based upon belief rather than truth – in effect destroying the cosmic order of the universe and causing the definitions of reality to fluctuate.

20.   What trio of time travelers were literally obliterating the Earth in thirty-thousand year cycles moving backwards through time?

Answer

The Time Twisters – Originally created by The One Who Remains, the last survivor of an ultimate time agency known as the Time Variance Authority, the Time Twisters were flawed in their creation and determined that they would set out on a quest for the beginning of creation, moving a destructive backwards arch that would intercept the Earth every thirty thousand years and obliterate it – until Thor and his allies traveled to the end of time to prevent their being created altogether.

21.   Who attempted to make his tiny isolated
        nation a world power through the creation of a
        supersonic bomb?

Answer

Bito Wladon, aka, Sonar I - Wladon was not only born ostracized for being the son of deaf parents (which was considered a mark of Satan to his superstitious countrymen) but when he managed to create a nucleo sonic motor that could utilize any sound as a weapon, his internal inferiority about himself and his country influenced him to use the technology to create a bomb that would make his native country of Mordora the most powerful in the world.

22.   What United States Marshall tracked a serial killer through remote bases in Anatarctica?

Answer

Carrie Stetko – The limited series "Whiteout" tells the story of Stetko's pursuit of a faceless foe in a fur hat from one murder scene to another as she endeavors to enforce her turf in the frozen terrain controlled by the largest US interest on the continent of Antarctica, McMurdo Base.

23.　　　What half-demonic heroine was stabbed in the back by the demon that possessed her?

Answer

Satana Hellstrom - A half-human daughter of the demon who called himself Satan, Satana was bonded with the demon Basilisk to increase her power, but she rebelled against her father and sought to form meaningful relationships with humans rather than feed off of them, until the Basilisk managed to curse Doctor Strange with lycanthropy in order to escape his confinement, though in attempting to kill his vessel, he ended up killing himself as well since their life forces remained bonded after being physically separated.

24.   What villain's career began when he received a box containing the severed hands of his father?

Answer

Temugin – Temugin was the estranged son of the arch-villain known as the Mandarin, but when his father died in battle against Iron Man, his severed hands were delivered to his son – complete with the ten rings that had given the Mandarin his powers – and Temugin found himself reluctantly thrust into the honor-bound duty of avenging his father's death.

25.   What device was responsible for genetically altering an alien race to make it impossible for them to leave their native planet?

Answer

The Eradicator – Originally a Kryptonian superweapon, the Eradicator was responsible for genetically altering Kryptonian physiology to make it fatal for any native of Krypton to leave their planet – in essence creating a rigidly imposed isolationism for Krypton – until Jor-El overcomes the defect through altering the DNA of his son, Kal-El that that he can survive the planet's destruction.

26.   What superhero actually chose the name of his career as his super alter ego?

Answer

Fred Drake, aka, Stuntman – Drake was the sole survivor of an acrobat trio known as the Flying Apollos, but when investigating the murders of his partners, he became employed as a stuntman for an actor, Don Daring – only when he got this job, he was inspired to take it one step further in actually choosing to become a superhero named – you guessed it – The Stuntman (because that's not conspicuous, at all).

27.   What was formed by the spawning of the
first Man of Lineage?

Answer

Nexus of Reality, aka, Nexus of All Realities – An unnamed creator deity made a woman named Cleito to represent the nature of all reality, who herself spawned the first Man of Lineage, Adam K'ad-Mon, and in doing so created the Nexus of Realities, a focal point that united all dimensions, created upon the very site of K'ad-Mon's birth.

28.   Who briefly adopted the ward of a wealthy millionaire in order to compel a marriage into the Bat Family?

Answer

Natalia Knight, aka, Nocturna – As part of a scheme to fund a lush lifestyle previously maintained through criminal activity, Knight filed adoption papers for Jason Todd when Bruce Wayne's guardianship was challenged – with the intent of offering Wayne to save himself legal struggles by letting her adoption go through, and to marry her afterwards.

29.   What hero was born when the New York Police Department refused to let him testify against the shooters of his wife and children?

Answer

Francis Castiglione, aka, Frank Castle, aka, the Punisher – After witnessing his family gunned down for witnessing a mob killing on the Sheep's Meadow Green in Central Park, Castle was denied any form of vengeance through the legal system since the New York Police Department at the time was heavily infiltrated by the Mafia, who refused to have any investigation against their membership pursued, which served as a catalyst for Castle taking law into his own hands as the Punisher.

30.   Who befriended a cosmic entity who came to Earth to learn about humanity, though was abandoned when she helped a superteam ambush him?

Answer

Tabitha Smith, aka, Time Bomb, aka, Boom Boom, aka, Meltdown – Tabitha was a runaway who encountered the Beyonder in the early days of his sojourn to Earth and traveled with him for a time on several cosmic quests, but when she was convinced to help the Avengers ambush him, she ran away yet again when she learned that the Beyonder felt betrayed by his "only friend" – and without any wonder, the Beyonder let her go.

31.   What villain themes his crimes around the day they are committed?

Answer

Julian Gregory Day, aka, Calendar Man – With a name that is even played off of the Julian and Gregorian calendars, is it any wonder that when Julian turned to a life of crime, that he chose to theme his activities around specific days, including seasons, holidays and even days of the week.

32.   What vampire hunter's ancestors changed
their name to avoid the unwanted association
with the Lord of Vampires?

Answer

Frank Drake – Descending from one of Vlad
Dracula's wives before he had become a vampire,
Drake's family amassed a substantial fortune, though
chose to change the family's name to hide their
connection to the ancient vampire lord – though
ironically, they kept Dracula's castle in their family,
until Frank Drake traveled there with plans of selling
the ancient edifice and inadvertently assisted in
resurrecting his ancestor.

33.   What god was cloned from a small fragment of his DNA recovered from an archaeological site in 1874?

Answer

Rama - Dr. Shyama Bhalla was given the DNA of the god, Rama, that was recovered as an artifact from an 1874 dig in order to clone the god in modern day, though it was not entirely for altruistic reasons - since the dark, sinister man she worked for was not only immortal, but apparently wanted the cloned god's power to spark an apocalypse.

34.   What rock singer found himself transported to an alternate sword and sorcery dimension after entering a run-down New York shop?

Answer

Jim Rook, aka, Nightmaster – Rook was the lead singer for the band "the Electrics" before finding himself transported to the mysterious land of Myrra after entering the run-down shop known as Oblivion, Inc, where he learned he was the descendant of an ancient Myrran hero, Nacht, and after taking up his ancestor's sword, became a hero there in his own right.

35.   Who   was   punished   for   speaking
blasphemy   when   she   told   her   headmistress
about her first manifestation of mutant power?

Answer

Jeanne-Marie Beaubier, aka, Aurora - Jeanne-
Marie was miserable being raised in the strict religious
school, Madama DuPont's School for Girls in Quebec,
but when she attempted to commit suicide at thirteen,
she perceived the manifestation of her powers of super
speed flight as a divine miracle - yet when she
confessed of this "divine" blessing, the sisters at the
school severely beat her for her pride, an event that
initiated a split personality in the fragile girl's psyche.

36.   Who took on a sidekick so she could get publicity in his journal?

Answer

Bonnie King, aka, Miss Arrowette - Though considered as much a nuisance as actual help, King took her Olympics-level archery into the realm of superheroes by trying to help out the Green Arrow and Speedy in Star City, though with a decidedly more feminine take to her trick arrows, eventually taking on a sidekick of her own, Bernell Jones, aka, Bowstring, just so that he would promote her in his published journal.

37.   Who was said to have been born inside a mountain of iron ore?

Answer

Joe Magarac, aka, The Genie of Steel – Magarac was actually a folk hero of Pittsburgh area steel mills, though many have contested that his creation was that of newspapermen – rather than actual folk tales – in an effort to create a hero to be looked up to be steel workers, making him an ideal candidate for comic adaptation by 1950 when the U.S. Steel Corp published "Joe the Genie of Steel #0".

38.   Who was the first black woman to receive her own self-named series?

Answer

Kate Williams, aka, Captain Confederacy II – In an alternate reality where the South won the U.S. Civil War, Williams was the wife of the original Captain Confederacy, and when her husband took on the identity of Kid Dixie, she took up his unused name, continuing as the first black woman to have a title named after herself – ironically enough, pregnant with the original Captain's baby during the entire time.

39.   Who was dropped as a living weapon against an invasion of Black Lanterns?

Answer

Vice – Vice was one of the most vicious members of the Red Lantern Corp who was captured and detained in the Green Lanterns' science cells on Oa, until the Black Lanterns invaded Oa and tried to consume the Green Lanterns' primary battery, prompting Kyle Rainer and Guy Gardner to drop Vice's cell on the Black Lanterns, counting on the savage Red Lantern to blindly obliterate the invading undead lanterns.

40.   What project is designed to illustrate how deformed and hyper-sexualized women are in comics?

Answer

The Hawkeye Initiative – Founded on December 2, 2012, the Hawkeye Initiative was created to raise awareness of how impossibly contorted women's bodies are portrayed in comics through a very simple formula: to fix any strong female character's pose, simply replace it with Hawkeye doing the same thing.

41.   What supervillain's base of operations is a
110 room castle built in the 16th century?

Answer

Castle Doom – Victor Von Doom conquered his
native land of Latveria early in his career, renaming
the capital of Hassenstadt to Doomstadt, and renaming
his infamous seat of power to Castle Doom.

42.   Who was best known for being powered by a kryptonite heart?

Answer

John Corben, aka, Metallo – Though Corben's origins have been shifted around through the years, the one consistent piece of his origin that has remained true is that Corben acquired kryptonite as his internal power source after his brain was transferred into an artificial metal body – something he continually used as a weapon against Superman.

43.   Who stole the serum that gave him super powers from a business partner he framed for embezzlement?

Answer

Norman Osborn, aka, Green Goblin I - Though Osborn himself is accredits himself with creating the Goblin Formula through the years, the truth is that he stole the formula from his business partner, Mendel Stromm, after Osborn framed the scientist for embezzlement from their co-owned company - a critical mistake, since when Osborn attempted to create the formula from Stromm's notes, it exploded in his face, granting him great power at the cost of his eroding sanity.

44.   Who fell victim to Kurdish Revolutionaries while searching for his parents in Turkey?

Answer

Jiro Manabe – In the series, Rebel Sword, young Jiro went to Turkey to meet his mother and find his long-lost father, only to find himself instead the embodiment of a Kurdish prophecy – the Rebel Sword.

45.   What splinter group of the Knights Templar created a series of subliminally conditioned superhuman champions?

Answer

The Order of St. Dumas – Originally part of the Knights Templar, the Order went underground after breaking away from the Catholic Church under the leadership of their founder, Dumas, and become dedicated to visiting wrath upon infidel foes of the faith, going so far as to create a generational superhuman agent to kill anyone who breached the Order's highly coveted secrecy – Azrael.

46.   What group consisted of cybernetically enhanced deceased offspring of a half-Asgardian?

Answer

The Endless Knights – Agamemnon was the sire of countless children through the centuries of his immortal life, but unknown to the rest of his organization known as the Pantheon, when one of his children died, he cybernetically enhanced their bodies to come to his aid upon command – essentially creating an army of undead demigods answerable to his sole will.

47.   What group of metahumans hailing from Florida swamps embodies the worst Southern stereotypes?

Answer

The Rednex – Seemingly all related, the Rednex are a group of metahumans who reside in the swamps of Chattahoochee, Florida, and proudly embrace their stereotypes, including inbreeding, missing teeth, banjo playing and cousin kissing.

48.   What district attorney's secretary became a superheroine with a bullwhip for a weapon?

Answer

Ginny Spears, aka, Veiled Avenger – Though only making four appearances, Spears made her mark on comics by possibly being the first representation of a woman with anger management issues, and a complete lack of concern for using her whip to force her opponents to shoot themselves.

49.   What alien species conquered worlds by genetically bonding native DNA with their own imprinted DNA in eggs?

Answer

Plodex – The Plodex were a warlike race that grew impatient with conquest through war and devised a radical means of universal conquest – to imprint their own DNA into eggs that were sent out across the galaxy in spacecraft programmed to summon native lifeforms to be dissected, then the native DNA harvested to be bonded with that of the Plodex in eggs that were then ejected with programmed instincts to conquer the world they were on.

50.   What character was created partially in parody to classic Charles Atlas ads?

Answer

Flex Mentallo – Charles Atlas was a body builder who advertised through comics from the 1940s into the 1980s, purporting to turn a 97 pound weakling into a muscle bound champion through offering a "free" book on dynamic tension – a sequence Grant Morrison parodied with Flex Mentallo, who likewise was a 97 pound weakling before a man with a television for a head gave him the free book which turned him into a muscle-bound hero.

51.   Who gained the powers of a spider from an ancient yogi?

Answer

Pavitr Prabhaar, aka, Spider-man (India) – Told as an Indian parallel to the American version, *Spider-man: India* was the story of young Pavitr, a grad student who moved to Mumbai when he received a partial scholarship, a trip that by chance brings him into contact with an ancient yogi, who grants him the powers of a spider so as to fight the evil that threatens the world.

52.   What fortress exists outside conventional space and time, though has an earthly anchor in Salem, Massachusetts?

Answer

The Tower of Fate – Created to serve as a safe haven for the various hosts of the Fate persona, the Tower of Fate is virtually impregnable with no doors or windows and rests on the Nexus of the Subtle Realms and therefore exists in no specific time or place, though it most often appears in a wooded area on the outskirts of Salem as its anchor in our reality.

53.   What caveman gained immortality after being bathed in the radiation of a meteorite?

Answer

Vandar Adg, aka, Vandal Savage – Though Vandal Savage has plagued the Earth since the beginning of recorded human history, he is actually considerably older – having been the leader of the Cro-Magnon Blood Tribe before being bathed in the radiation of a mysterious meteorite that increased his intellect and gave him immortality.

54.   What was the first crossover event exclusive to annuals?

Answer

The Evolutionary War – Though extended crossovers were commonplace, one had never been attempted to be told exclusively through annual publications before the Evolutionary War, the story of the High Evolutionary's efforts to accelerate human evolutions and to remove impurities from the human genome, which of course was opposed by the entirety of the Marvel Universe, heroes and villains alike.

55.   What superhumanly fast hero is apparently so well known that he is even listed in the phone book?

Answer

Maxwell the Mighty – Maxwell was a golden aged hero billed as the 1000 Horse Power Human who not only had the unique trait of uttering unusual words like "Jemima" while fighting, but also had no concern of being found out since he had his superhero identity actually listed in the phone book, making him easily reachable by people needing his help.

56.   What series of superhero teams was inspired by a pair of Kryptonian gods?

Answer

Nightwing and Flamebird - Nightwing and Flamebird were originally a pair of Kryptonian deities who were symbolized by being killed, reborn and needing to find each other again in each rebirth - a unity that inspired several teams named after them, beginning with Superman and Jimmy Olson in Kandor, though possibly the most well-known appearance being of Dick Grayson and Bette Kane.

57.   Who inadvertently destroyed a villain's asteroid base while traveling to Earth?

Answer

Warlock – A member of the techno-organic race known as the Technarchy, Warlock fled from his own people when he refused to drain the lifeglow of sentient beings, but his mad flight was so reckless, that he collided with Asteroid M upon entering Earth's atmosphere, destroying the headquarters of the mutant villain, Magneto.

58.   What alternate reality group of former heroes tried to destroy their Prime Earth counterparts in their quest to kill an Eternal?

Answer

The Gatherers – The Gatherers were actually all sole survivors of their own respective worlds, as well as being surviving members of their own realities' Avengers, tricked into believing that the Eternal, Sersi, had gone mad and destroyed their worlds – prompting a misguided quest into destroying the "prime" Sersi on Earth 616, and killing their "prime" counterparts to prevent being destroyed by cellular breakdown for occupying the same dimension as their duplicates.

59.   What super group consists of third-rate superheroes billed as eternal teenagers of the future?

Answer

Super Duper – In a world where superheroes have become corrupted by their celebrity, putting the world more at risk than not through their reckless behavior, the CIA formed its own groups of heroes to monitor the superhero populace, but those who are considered less-than-spectacular for marketability purposes get sent to the third-string group known as Super Duper.

60.   Whose master thesis was on the effects of superheroes on society?

Answer

Jesse Chambers, aka, Jesse Quick – Though her father, Johnny Quick, had taught her his secret formula for super speed, Jesse elected instead initially to continue with her schooling rather than take up being a costumed hero, even going so far as to entitle her thesis, "The Impact of Superheroes on Society".

61.   What alien race taught a despotic villain the technology necessary to transfer one's consciousness into another body?

Answer

The Ovoids - When Doctor Doom was left floating in space following a defeat by the Fantastic Four, he was rescued by the alien Ovoids, who mistakenly provided Doom with access to their advanced technology without realizing his evil nature, including to the ability to transfer his consciousness into another body - which of course Doom wasted no time in using to take the place of Mister Fantastic.

62.   What villain was born with an extreme case of epidermolytic hyperkeratosis?

Answer

Waylon Jones, aka, Killer Croc – Though Croc is known to possess above average strength and reflexes that are possibly the result of some form of regressive atavism, his most remarkable feature is his scale-like skin that was the result of a defect that gave him scaly, patchy skin since birth, a defect that increased the toughness of his skin so that eventually he could even deflect bullets from a distance.

63.   What fortress exists at the last nanosecond before entropy ends the universe?

Answer

Vanishing Point – Originally the home of Booster Gold, his wife and son, Rip Hunter, Vanishing Point was sent to the end of time as the one place Booster's enemies could not find them, creating a headquarters in the "future" for the Linear Men as a locality that existed outside the normal flow of time, permitting them to monitor all of time and space for time paradoxes they could police and resolve.

64.   What alien superteam was created with deliberate resemblance to another publisher's 30th century team of alien heroes?

Answer

Imperial Guard – Introduced in X-Men #107, the Imperial Guard was a collective team of alien heroes in defense of the Shi'ar Empire, though their creator Dave Cockrum intentionally created a resemblance between the alien team to that of DC's Legion of Superheroes, a series he had previously been well-known for working on.

65.   Who was raised to serve an anti-matter entity seeking to destroy the multiverse?

Answer

Baroness Paula Von Gunther, aka, Dark Angel, aka, Donna Troy (Earth 7) - Dark Angel was revealed to be an alternate version of Donna Troy, who herself was a clone of Princess Diana of Themyscira, rescued as a child by the Anti-Monitor, who used her as a servant to his plans to destroy the multiverse much as his positive-universe counterpart, Monitor, rescued and used Harbinger to advance his plans to save it.

66.   What mutant laid six eggs after being impregnated by a fellow student?

Answer

Angel Salvadore, aka, Tempest – Angel originally kissed her fellow student, Beak, on a bet, but when true romantic feelings developed between them, they slept together – an act that resulted in a pregnancy accelerated by her mutant-fly physiology and her laying six eggs in Wolverine's old shed, eggs that later hatched into babies that shared Beak's chicken and Angel's fly physiologies.

67.   What team is formed after the world's preeminent superteam are all killed when their headquarters is blown up?

Answer

Hero Alliance – The Guardsmen was the primary superteam of the world, but when the team is killed by simple bombs planted in their headquarters, Victor – a former member who resigned over what he considered a lack of moral standards in newer members – takes it upon himself to act as a mentor to less experienced yet powerful heroes left in the world.

68.   What substance – originally introduced in a television series – can split certain heroes into good and evil counterparts?

Answer

Black Kryptonite – Black kryptonite was originally used in the Smallville television series against Clark Kent, but when it was introduced in the normal comic books, it was used by Lex Luthor against Supergirl, splitting her into two separate people with diverse morals – the good counterpart dressed in Supergirl's original costume, while her evil counterpart appeared in a black and white version.

69.   Who was the first foe of the original gamma-irradiated hero?

Answer

Yuri Topolov, aka, Gargoyle - An atomic accident led to Yuri being grossly mutated into a dwarf with oversized head and increased intelligence, but when he heard of the Hulk, he captured the emerald goliath in hopes of learning how radiation had instead created a superhuman versus his own gross deformity - a gambit that worked, since Bruce Banner was able to use gamma radiation to cure Yuri, though it did not spare his passing his deformity genetically to his son, the Gremlin.

70.   What force was responsible for creating the potential of superhumans during its second pass through the universe?

Answer

The Godwave – The Source being the consciousness of the DC Universe, it was responsible for sending out a cosmic force of divine energy knows as the Godwave that created the seeds of divinity in its first pass through the universe, but when it reached the edge of the universe, it rebounded with lesser power that created the potential for superhumans on worlds such as Earth.

71.   What hero used a magic amulet to travel through time to recover rare works of art?

Answer

Aaron Piper, aka, Spookman – When museum owner and former archaeologist Piper discovered the Moonstone Amulet, it transformed him into the Spookman, with the ability to travel through time – an ability he did not use to specifically fight crime, but instead sought to travel through time to preserve rare works of art for posterity.

72.   Who relocated a stolen mountain into the middle of Los Angeles?

Answer

Jaard, aka, Starseed – Jaard's people lived in their mountain caves before aliens stole their mountain into space, prompting the peaceful people to overcome the aliens in order to seize the advanced technology to return their mountain home – only all of Jaard's people died during the return voyage, leaving Jaard alone to master the dreamtime and transforming into the golden, angelic form of the Starseed.

73.   What hero was created by the fusing of a scientist's mind with a redesigned world conquering virus mutated cyborg?

Answer

Salah Miandad, aka, ReMAC – When a partially active remnant of the OMAC Project is discovered by the Justice League, Batman tricked his teammates to seize the cyborg for himself in order to create a tool to be used by the Outsiders for infiltration, but when Miandad working as an assistant tried to create a new interface, he was knocked into a coma and ended up having his mind fused with the ReMAC unit.

74. What alternate future universe was spawned from an initial *What If* storyline?

Answer

MC2 (Marvel Comics 2) Universe, aka, Earth #982 – In a universe where May Parker, the daughter of Spider-man and Mary Jane Watson, survived as told in *What If* (vol 2) #105, she grew to become part of a future universe of heroes – including future versions of the Avengers (A2), X-Men (X-People) and various other individual heroes who were either the children of or inspired by heroes of modern day.

75.   What hero retrieved a medieval suit of armor from a castle in France to carry on the legacy of a hero from Charlemagne's time?

Answer

Captain Robert Britain, aka, Iron Ace – When Britain is shot down over France, he took refuge in the castle of the resistance leader, Dr. LaFarge, but when the doctor is himself killed by Nazis, Britain dons the armor of a Charlemagne-aged hero known as the Iron Ace to carry the battle to the villains, including taking to the sky in full armor to do battle with the enemies of freedom thereafter.

76.   Whose base of operations is on an asteroid between the orbit of Mars and Jupiter?

Answer

Rick Starr, aka, Space Ranger - Hiding behind a seemingly shiftless persona as an executive in his father's multi-million dollar company, Rick moonlighted as the space-faring hero, Space Ranger, in the 22nd Century, utilizing his vast fortune to not only fund his quest to protect Earth from futuristic threats, but also to outfit a base of operations on a secret asteroid located in orbit between Mars and Jupiter.

77.   Who is considered the modern nexus being of the central universe of reality?

Answer

Wanda Maximoff, aka, Scarlet Witch – A nexus being is a rare individual who embodies a realm's character and serves as a focal point for reality, a concept Wanda embodied through her reality manipulating mutant abilities that gave her the capability to affect probabilities and thus shape the present as well as the future.

78.   Who was killed by a car ten years before he would gain the time traveling powers that made him a threat to his murderer?

Answer

Walker Gabriel, aka, Chronos II – Walker took possession of his predecessor David Clint's research in time travel, and became the second Chronos, a sometimes hero and sometimes thief, though when his activities posed a threat to Per Degaton's plans, the villainous time traveler had young Walker killed by a car at the age of ten, thus eliminating the possibility of his growing to become the second Chronus.

79.   Who abandoned her mystically-granted powers of leadership to spare the lives of other mystically powered beings?

Answer

Heather Hudson, aka, Guardian, aka, Vindicator - As part of a scheme to transform the world, Loki created a Fire Fountain capable of transforming people into demi-gods - but as all things with Loki, there was a trick in that not only was it powered by the magics of world, but it would kill anyone with natural magical abilities, a sacrifice Hudson could not accept, surrendering her own powers gained from the fountain in order to save the lives of her teammates who had magical powers.

80.   What was the first comic to have its #0 issue printed as a card set?

Answer

Plasm, aka, Warriors of Plasm – Jim Shooter had a unique idea when he decided to launch his new comic company, Defiant Comics, with prelude issues as a set of collectible cards that could be assembled to read the actual comic itself when inserted in 9 pocket album pages – though unfortunately what could have a milestone in comic history was sunk by a vindictive Marvel Comics who sued the fledgling publisher out of business.

81.   What superhero was modeled after Woody Allen?

Answer

Myron Victor, aka, Merryman - In a self-parody of DC heroes and their legacy, the Inferior Five were led by Myron in the roll of Merryman, a second generation hero whose sole power seemed to be the awareness of just how foolish he was in leading a team of misfits, choosing to dress as a high strung 98 pound weakling in a jester costume whose resemblance to Woody Allen was not only unmistakable, but deliberate.

82.   What prosecutor-turned-crimefighter put himself out of a job?

Answer

Brian Butler, aka, Mr. Scarlet – Butler first took up being the Red Knight of Justice because he could not bear being unable to put away all criminals, but he was so effective as a midnight crimefighter, that he literally put himself out of a job as a prosecutor – so that he had to instead spend his days looking for odd jobs while he continued his nighttime vigilantism.

83.   Who plucked out his own right eye in order to gain supreme power over manipulating the energy of power gems?

Answer

Occulus – In a microscopic universe known as the Inniverse, a war between two brother worlds ended in the destruction in one that left a ring of crystal fragments around the surviving world, crystals that could be manipulated by certain residents of the planet below, including Occulus, who actually cut out his own right eye in order to increase his power not only to control the gems' energy, but through that energy in ruling his homeworld.

84.   Whose body was looted to create a giant tuning fork capable of altering reality?

Answer

The Anti-Monitor – In a quest to undo the events of the Crisis On Infinite Earths, where the multiverse was merged into a single Earth, Superboy Prime located the desiccated corpse of the Anti-Monitor and used it to create a massive structure capable of creating new Earth variations, all in hopes of recreating the Earth from which he himself originated.

85.   Who gained super powers by drinking an enchanted potion added to his water in a prison commissary?

Answer

Carl "Crusher" Creel, aka, the Absorbing Man – While serving time in prison for his part in an extortion racket, Creel caught the eye of the Asgardian, Loki, who secreted a potion of rare Asgardian herbs into the convicts water, which thereafter gave Creel the powers to absorb any substance he touched – a presumably perfect ability to fight on Loki's behalf against Thor.

86.   What device was used to turn a superteam into heroes nobody knew in order to defeat their evil counterparts?

Answer

H-Dial – A mysterious device that can transform anyone into into a hero by pressing the letters "H-E-R-O" on a dial-like device, the H-Dial was most commonly used by normal people to become heroes from other universes, but when the Justice League needed to defeat the Injustice League imbued with cosmic power, they used the device to become new heroes the villains did not know how to defeat.

87.   Whose transformed shape's orange hair turned white when his spirit took over the deceased body of a teammate?

Answer

Walter Langowski, aka, Wanda Langowski, aka, Sasquatch – Walter died after his transformed body as the hero Sasquatch was revealed to be a conduit for the Great Beast, Tanaraq, and his teammate Snowbird was forced to kill him, though ironically enough, when Snowbird herself died, his spirit took her body and used her transforming powers to resume his Sasquatch (but not his male) form, though with white fur rather than orange.

88.   What legal authority was passed by Franklin D. Roosevelt to draft superheroes?

Answer

Article X – Originally created during World War II to form the All-Star Squadron, Article X is an executive order that has the authority to draft superheroes into military service during times of need, most recently used to gather heroes against the threat of the Gods of Apokalips during the Final Crisis.

89.   Who devised a strategy to defeat an emerald monster through showing him love and affection?

Answer

Colonel Cary St Lawrence – A military officer and heir to General "Thunderbolt" Ross' military mission to defeat the Hulk, St. Lawrence eventually determined that the Hulk was like a child who just did not know how to get affection in a positive way, concluding that the best way to control the Hulk is to give him the trust and affection he so desperately craves.

90.   What supervillain-turned-hero used an exoskeleton suit and other equipment to simulate arachnid-like powers?

Answer

The Spider – Originally a criminal mastermind, the Spider grew bored with being a criminal – in particular in fighting other criminals for gain – and decided to instead become a hero, using his fights to overcome criminals to better society rather than himself, using an amazing array of equipment that allowed him to shoot webs, never lose his balance and to swing from building to building.

91.   What iconic hero was originally conceived as a bald telepathic villain bent on world domination?

Answer

Superman – When Jerry Siegel and Joe Schuster – then high school students – first collaborated on the concept of Superman, they introduced him as a telepathic villain in the pages of *Science Fiction: The Advance Guard of Civilization* #3, with this incarnation bearing a striking resemblance to the future hero's later arch-nemesis, Lex Luthor.

92.   What organization serves as the mutant equivalent of Doctors Without Borders?

Answer

Mutants Sans Frontières – Though the name translates to Mutants Without Borders, the organization was founded by Warren Worthington III, aka, Angel, who has used the nonprofit organization to not only reach out to mutants in need around the world, but also to covertly fund various teams of X-Men.

93.   What family of androids each contains a portion of the power of a nuclear bomb?

Answer

The Nuclear Family – A group of androids first encountered by the Outsiders, this set of androids is programmed to personify the Ozzy and Harriet style 1950s family – with the exception that Dad emits radiation, Mom gives off electromagnetic pulses, Biff (the eldest son) uses a thermal pulse, Brat (the youngest son) shares the power to transform into radioactive fallout with the family dog, and Sis can produce a destructive blast.

94.   What super robot traveled with two kids who could transform into super versions of themselves?

Answer

Zor – This Mexican superhero robot was created by an unnamed professor to be a nearly indestructible defender of endangered citizens, and chose to go adventuring with the professor's son and daughter, who themselves were capable of transforming themselves into a super girl and super boy whenever danger was near.

95.   What mutant is also the sometimes–ruler of a demonic dimension?

Answer

Illyana Rasputina, aka, Magic – Originally kidnapped to the dimension of Limbo by Belasco in a scheme to awaken the elder gods, the plan backfired when young Illyana drove the demon lord from his own dimension and seized control as his heir, and though she has died and been reborn since, the mutant known as the Demonchild continues to hold dominion over her former prison.

96.   What character's comic series was promoted in a distributor's catalog with a "life-size" image of the her breasts?

Answer

Desiree Hopewell, aka, Fatale – Jim Shooter created the character of Fatale primarily in response to the popular voluptuous female characters popular in the 1990's, going so far as to not only poke fun at the concept, but also to emphasize the excessive breast size in several ways, including advertising her self-named series by running a large full-sized image of her (clothed) breasts as advertisement for the series itself.

97.   What former alien ruler became worshiped as a goddess after she was turned into a being of pure energy?

Answer

X'hal – X'hal was ruler of the planet Okaara when she was kidnapped and forced to endure torturous scientific experiments by the amoral reptilian race known as the Psions, a process that first killed her but later created a metamorphosis that turned her into pure energy with power not only sufficient to obliterate her tormentors, but to also return to her home planet to be worshiped as a goddess.

98.   What villain was retconned to be part of an alien plot prior to his actual appearance in comics?

Answer

Quentin Beck, aka, Mysterio – Although the master of illusion himself did not appear in costume until *Amazing Spider-man* #13 (1964), it was later retconned that an alien plot Spider-man had foiled back in *Amazing Spider-man* #2 (1963) had actually been Mysterio and his gang in disguise.

99.   Whose first appearance is better known for being the first story allowed to involve narcotics under the Comic Code Authority?

Answer

Boston Brand, aka, Deadman – Brand was killed by a mysterious character known only as the Hook and granted an afterlife as a ghost capable of possessing living people in order to track down his killer, but his origin story is better known for his first act as a hero being to stop the distribution of "snow" through his circus, a sensitive drug-related concept that had previously been banned by the CCA.

100.   What comic book company distinguished
        itself by publishing double-sized comic books
        during its five year life?

Answer

Tower Comics – Though Tower Comics was only
in operation from 1964 through 1965, they were
known as something of a throwback to the Golden Age
(which ended in 1950) for not only publishing 64-
page issues at a time when 32 pages was the norm, but
also for printing multiple stories in the same volume,
with all the characters uniting in the final story of each
issue.

101.   What powerful witch took on the role of a governess in order to protect the first child of a superteam?

Answer

Agatha Harkness – Agatha was a powerful witch who was over 500 years old when she abandoned her leadership over New Salem, Colorado, to care for special children in need, and though she had retired from this occupation, she readily agreed to act as governess for Franklin Richards, once she considered his potential as the child of Mr. Fantastic and the Invisible Girl.

102.   What 7th Dimension escapee tried to conquer the Earth by destroying all plant life?

Answer

Star Sapphire – The character who would evolve to become a persistent opponent of the Silver Age Green Lantern actually premiered as an opponent of the Golden Age Flash, having escaped from where she had been imprisoned in the 7th Dimension by the Zamarons and attempted to take over the Earth by destroying all plant life in order to deplete the world of oxygen.

103.   Whose diminished stature is the result of using his body to contain the spirit of an evil sorcerer?

Answer

Eugene Judd, aka, Puck – Best known for his heroic acts as a member of both Beta and Alpha Flight teams, Eugene began his career as a thief, though when a misguided theft of the Black Blade of Baghdad resulted in freeing the evil spirit of the ancient sorcerer Black Raazer, he began his heroic career with the self-sacrifice of using his own body to imprison the evil spirit, an effect that reduced him in size and stature forever after.

104.   What sidekick originally required to be "magnetized" every time he and his hero went to fight crime?

Answer

Davey Landis, aka, Davey – Somewhat common for the Golden Age era, Davey used his own first name when he fought beside his hero, Magno the Magnet Man, though in order to fight crime, he initially required a magnetic charge from his hero to provide him a portion of Magno's own magnetic powers – though eventually Davey was able to use the powers on his own without being magnetized by Magno beforehand.

105.   What champion of the multiverse served as the Amazons's official historian in her final days?

Answer

Lyla Michaels, aka, Harbinger – Lyla was originally introduced as a servant of the Monitor just prior to the Crisis on Infinite Earths, and later became a champion in defense of the multiverse against the Anti-Monitor, though she eventually settled on Themyscira, home of the Amazons, where she served as their official historian before being slain by the forces of Darkseid.

106.   Who was the first new member inducted into the Legion of Superheroes after it was founded?

Answer

Clark Kent, aka, Superboy – The Legion of Superheroes was originally founded upon the ideals set down through the legend of Superboy, and it's founding members – Cosmic Boy, Saturn Girl and Lightning Lad – made a point to travel back to the 20th Century to make sure their first new member would be the one who had inspired them in the first place – Superboy!

107.   What group of heroes were the time paradox duplicates of their original counterparts?

Answer

Batch SW6, aka, the Legionaires – Though "Legionaire" is often used as a term for any member of the Legion of Superheroes, the team known as the Legionnaires consisted of a group of Legion duplicates originally thought to be clones of original Legion of Superheroes members, though it was later discovered that they were actually time displaced duplicates created by the Time Trapper.

108. Who was believed responsible for ordering a Legion member to destroy an entire planet of sentient beings?

Answer

Rokk Krinn, aka, Cosmic Boy – In a seemingly vicious move to protect the universe from the Dominators, Cosmic Boy order Mon El – dying from lead poisoning – to fly into the heart of the Dominator's planet with a bomb to destroy it – though in reality, it was a Phantom Zone projector which actually transported the Dominator's and their world into the Phantom Zone, kept a secret to prevent anyone from freeing them afterwards.

109.   What Legion of Superheroes member discovered that the girl he was dating was actually a man taking a sex change drug?

Answer

Jan Arrah, aka, Element Lad – Jan's girlfriend, Shvaughn, was actually born a man named Sean, but had his sex changed with a futuristic drug known as ProFem, though when the drug became unavailable and he reverted back to male, Jan professed that he still loved him in spite of the drug, not because of it.

110.   Who was the son of the Legion of
        Superheroes' financier?

Answer

Reep Daggle, aka, Chameleon Boy, aka, Chameleon – Though RJ Brande was originally believed to be the human financier of the Legion, it was revealed later that not only was he a shape-shifting Durlan, but also the father of the Legion's member, Chameleon Boy!

111.   Who was responsible for locking a future
Legion of Superheroes member inside a reactor?

Answer

Zaxton Regulus, aka, Dr. Regulus – Regulus was experimenting radioactive gold when an unforeseen accident injured both him and Dirk Mogma, though he blamed Dirk for the accident and sought revenge against Dirk by locking him inside a nuclear reactor, an accident that inadvertently gave Dirk superpowers that he later used to become the Legion member, Sun Boy.

112.   What Legion of Superheroes member gained his powers after his ship was eaten by a giant space energy beast?

Answer

Jo Nah, aka, Ultra Boy – Jo was aboard a spaceship that swallowed by a giant space whale, and the energy inside the beast transformed his body so that he could assume a variety of superpowers, though only use one specific power at a time.

113.   Who killed one of the forms of a triplicate Legionaire?

Answer

Computo – Computo was an automated assistant created by Braniac 5, but it developed homicidal emotions and sought to raise an army of machines against the living beings of Earth, setting his sites initially on not only defeating the Legion and driving them from Metropolis, but also in killing one of Triplicate Girl's bodies, dooming her thereafter to be Duo Damsel.

114.   Who was expelled from the Legion of Superheroes for killing his girlfriend's ex-boyfriend in self-defense?

Answer

Thom Kallor, aka, Star Boy – The Legion has a long-standing rule against killing, and so even though he took the life of Dream Girl's ex-boyfriend in self-defense, the rule was so adamant that the members expelled Star Boy from the Legion for the offense.

115.   Who was the first homosexual couple within the ranks of the Legion of Superheroes?

Answer

Salu Digby and Ayla Ranzz, aka, Shrinking Violet and Lightning Lass – The two had been long-standing members of the Legion for years before their close working relationship eventually blossomed into an actual relationship in 1989.

116.   What structure was established from a second rocket sent to Earth by the last son of Krypton's father?

Answer

Legion Clubhouse - Jor-El had fashioned a second rocket designed to be sent after his son Kal-El's rocket ship, containing diapers, extra clothes, toys and a final message to their son - but it inexplicably arrived a thousand years behind Kal-El's rocket, and when the original Legion members discovered this upon gaining entry, they convinced their financier, R.J. Brande to buy and remodel the rocket as their headquarters, the Legion Clubhouse.

117.   Whose assassination attempt forged the members of the Legion of Superheroes into a team?

Answer

R.J. Brande – When millionaire R.J. Brande was visiting Earth, Saturn Girl detected a plot to kill him, and with the aid of Lightning Lad and Cosmic Lad, the three foiled the plot and forever earned Brande's appreciation – who went on to finance the three as a new super team who could work towards defending the Earth from imminent threats.

118.   What governing agency does the Legion of Superheroes report to?

Answer

United Planets – In the 30th and 31st Centuries, Earth is the center of a multiple world government known as the United Planets, who is the authority that both deputized the Legion as Earth's defenders and to whom the Legion ultimately answers to for authority.

119.   What Legion of Superheroes member hails from a planet that occupies the same space as Earth in another dimension?

Answer

Tinya Wazzo, aka, Phantom Girl, aka, Phase, aka, Apparition – Tinya is the only member of her planet, Bgztl, who can phase between her Fourth Dimension home to Earth, though when she phases, she can be seen in both worlds, which can add to some confusion about where she really is.

120.   Which Legion of Superheroes member was driven insane by using his powers to save the universe?

Answer

Tenzil Kem, aka, Matter-Eater Lad - Literally able to consume any form of matter, Tenzil saved the universe by eating the previously-believed indestructible Miracle Machine - a device capable of converting thought into reality - though the consumption of such a powerful device drove him insane for years.

121. What Legion of Superheroes member was transformed into a savage lycanthrope by exposure to a rare element?

Answer

Brin Londo, aka, Timber Wolf – Brin's father went in search of a rare element known as Zuunium in order to use it in a device designed to give his son superpowers, though the process was only partially successful, ending up reverting Brin into a semi-animalistic hero known for many years as the Lone Wolf, before joining the Legion as Timber Wolf.

122.   Who was sent to join the Legion of Superheroes, though he was actually evil and bent upon the Legion's destruction?

Answer

Hart Druiter, aka, Nemesis Kid, aka, Tarik the Mute – Hart applied for membership in the Legion and was initially accepted, but in reality he had been sent by the evil aliens, Khunds, to infiltrate the Legion, learn their secrets, and ultimately destroy the Legion from within.

123.   Who was the first Legionnaire to die?

Answer

Garth Ranzz, aka, Lightning Lad – Though he was revived only a handful of issues later, Lightning Lad gave his life in a battle with Zaryan, in spite of Saturn Girl's best efforts to prevent it.

124.   What Legion of Superheroes member was the son of Japan's greatest crime lord?

Answer

Val Amorr, aka, Karate Kid – Val's father was the Black Dragon, the greatest crime lord of Japan, who was in turn killed by Japan's greatest hero, Kirau Nezumi, who subsequently raised Val as his own son.

125.   What Legion of Superheroes member was actually the princess of her homeworld?

Answer

Princess Projectra, aka, Queen Projectra, aka, Sensor Girl – Projectra was actually the heir to throne of the low-tech world Orando, and though she served as a member of the Legion at various times, her loyalties to her homeworld created a rift between her homeworld and the Legion at various points in time, as well.

126. Who was responsible for changing the powers of a Legion of Superheroes member from lightning to making objects lightweight?

Answer

Nura Nal, aka, Dream Girl – When Nura's native precognitive abilities foresaw the deaths of several Legion members, she utilized her homeworld's science to alter the powers of Lightning Lass from her native ability to cast lightning bolts to having control over making object's lightweight, earning her the new name of Light Lass for several years thereafter.

127. Who gave his life to help being a Legionaire back to life?

Answer

Proty – A method was found to bring back the deceased Lightning Lad, but only at the cost of another's life, and so Proty – Chameleon Boy's shape-changing pet – took Saturn Girl's place in the ceremony so that it would be his life rather than one of the heroes that was lost in order to bring back the founding Legion member.

TO BE CONTINUED...

APPENDIX A

The Dead Wrong Answers

Since these questions were originally asked live, as part of a weekly contest, there were bound to be some that were simply Dead Wrong...

Question

What superteam consists of vampires who have overcome their need for human blood?

Answer

Spice Girls

Question

Who stole residual energy left over with people saved by a hero in order to resurrect his wife?

Answer

Obama

Question

What comic book romance inspired the wife of a rock star to attempt to make a television series out of the comic couple?

Answer

Tony Stark and Himself

Question

Who attempted to make his tiny isolated nation a world power through the creation of a supersonic bomb?

Answer

Sonic the Hedgehog

Question

What villain's career began when he received a box containing the severed hands of his father?

Answer

The Handfather

Question

What rock singer found himself transported to an alternate sword and sorcery dimension after entering a run-down New York shop?

Answer

Jack Black

Question

Who was dropped as a living weapon against an invasion of Black Lanterns?

Answer

The Anvil

Question

What project is designed to illustrate how deformed and hyper-sexualized women are in comics?

Answer

Sports Illustrated Swimsuit Issue

Question

Who gained the powers of a spider from an ancient yogi?

Answer

Boo-Boo

Question

What caveman gained immortality after being bathed in the radiation of a meteorite?

Answer

Captain Caveman

Question

What substance – originally introduced in a television series – can split certain heroes into good and evil counterparts?

Answer

Play-Doh

Question

What super group consists of third-rate superheroes billed as eternal teenagers of the future?

Answer

Bon Jovi

Question

Who is considered the modern nexus being of the central universe of reality?

Answer

Oprah

Question

Who abandoned her mystically-granted powers of leadership to spare the lives of other mystically powered beings?

Answer

Ayn Rand

Question

Who devised a strategy to defeat an emerald monster through showing him love and affection?

Answer

Dr. Phil

Question

Who devised a strategy to defeat an emerald monster through showing him love and affection?

Answer

Mrs. Hulk

Question

What comic book company distinguished itself by publishing double-sized comic books during its five year life?

Answer

The Comic Pusher

Question

What powerful witch took on the role of a governess in order to protect the first child of a superteam?

Answer

Witch of the Swamp

Question

What structure was established from a second rocket sent to Earth by the last son of Krypton's father?

Answer

Time Out Corner

Question

What Legion of Superheroes member hails from a planet that occupies the same space as Earth in another dimension?

Answer

Dimension Boy

About the Author

Ron Glick (born January 20, 1969) is a community activist, and is presently active in several charitable enterprises. He was born in Plainville, KS. After living in various states, he currently lives in Kalispell, MT. He is the author of The Godslayer Cycle, Chaos Rising and the Oz-Wonderland series, as well as having written several volumes of Ron El's Comic Book Trivia. He is presently working on the second novel of Chaos Rising, Immortal's Discord. He loves contact and welcomes input on his work through his website at http://ronglick.com.